This book is dedicated to my niece Ja'Myah La'Rhea Key and to all the little girls in the world. You can become anything that you want to be in life. Keep dreaming because the sky is the limit.

ISBN 9780982795088

Printed in the United States of America

The Adventures of Sugamama

By Shaneisha Dodson

Once upon a time, there was a beautiful little girl named Sugamama who loved to help her mother bake.

One night Sugamama ate so many cookies that she fell asleep with her apron on.

In the middle of the night, she heard a loud **boom** so she woke up.

To her surprise, her room was full of pink lights and green lights.

Sugamama got out of bed and looked in the mirror. Her apron had turned into a superhero cape, and her afro puffs were pink. She could not believe her eyes so she touched her hair to see if it was real.

Her afro puffs were magical. They gave her the ability to fly high into the sky.

She flew all over the world until...

She saw a little girl in a red house who was crying. The little girl looked scared so Sugamama flew to help her.

Sugamama asked, "Why are you crying?"

The little girl said, "There's a monster under my bed."

Sugamama looked under the bed. Two big eyes starred at her. She said, "I'm not scared of you."

She growled, and the monster ran out of the house.

The little girl said, "Thanks Sugamama, you saved me!"

Sugamama spent the rest of the night saving the world.

When Sugamama finished, she was so tired that she flew home, put a silk bonnet over her magical hair and fell sound asleep.

The End...

CPSIA information can be obtained
at www.ICGtesting.com
Printed in the USA
BVHW022057171120
593549BV00003B/118